Something Queer in Outer Space

Something Queer in Outer Space

by Elizabeth Levy

illustrated by Mordicai Gerstein

Hyperion Paperbacks for Children, New York

To Gwen, Jill, and Fletcher and to astronaut Pete Cooper,
who took the first sandwich into space
—E. L.

For Daisy: Welcome to this wonderfully queer and mysterious world
—M. G.

Text © 1993 Elizabeth Levy.
Illustrations copyright © 1993 Mordicai Gerstein.
All rights reserved.
Printed in the United States of America.
For information address Hyperion Books for Children,
114 Fifth Avenue, New York, New York 10011

First Hyperion Paperback edition: September 1993

1 3 5 7 9 10 8 6 4 2

ISBN: 1-56282-566-6 (trade)
1-56282-279-9 (pbk.)

LC#: 92-54870

Fletcher poked his nose out of the tent and looked up at
the stars. Gwen and her best friend, Jill, were camping
out in Jill's backyard.

"This is the life," said Gwen. It was great to be able to
sleep in a tent *and* order pizza. She fed a tiny piece of
pepperoni to Fletcher.

    "I can see the Milky Way," said Jill, pointing to a milky ribbon of stars. "There are so many mysteries in space."

    Gwen gazed up at the sky. "Nope, nothing queer going on up there," she said.

    "I don't mean 'mystery' like solving a crime," said Jill. "I mean it's just so *awesome.*"

    Gwen rolled over. "You're getting goopy. Leave the mysteries to me."

THE MILKY WAY

ANOTHER FIREFLY

    Fletcher's big basset-hound nose lifted high in the air. "Ow—wooo—ow—woooo," he howled.

    Gwen giggled. "I think he believes the moon is made of green cheese," she said.

    Jill put her arms around Fletcher. "You want to go up there, don't you, boy?" she whispered. "I read that they're looking for a dog to put into space."

(NOTE: A SHOOTING STAR IS A
METEOR THAT ENTERS EARTH'S
ATMOSPHERE AND BURNS UP.)

"Fletcher in space," guffawed Gwen. "Give me a break.
Fletcher doesn't like moving from your front steps."
Just then a shooting star blazed across the sky.
"Make a wish," said Gwen quickly.

Every day after that Jill waited for proof that her wish had come true, but the letter she was hoping for never came.

Then one afternoon, as Gwen and Jill walked home from school, a car pulled up in front of Jill's house. A man and a woman got out with a boy and a girl. The boy was holding the leash of a Yorkshire terrier wearing a muzzle. Fletcher wagged his tail. The little dog growled.

Fletcher hustled off the front steps. Fletcher *never* hustled.

Jill's mother came out to see what was going on.

"Good afternoon," said the woman. "I'm Ms. Watsuda. This is my son Willie, my daughter Risa, and this is Colonel John Castle."

"Monique Watsuda! You're an astronaut!" exclaimed Jill.

Ms. Watsuda smiled.

"Who's the dog?" asked Gwen.

"Fang," said Willie. "He's a space dog." Fang growled again.

"I was very moved by your letter," Ms. Watsuda said to Jill.

"What letter?" asked Jill's mother and Gwen in unison.

"I wrote to NASA," said Jill, "and I wished on a shooting star that Fletcher could go into space."

Fletcher wagged his tail.

Ms. Watsuda took out Jill's letter and read it aloud.

Everybody stared down at Fletcher, who had fallen asleep in a ball. "He does look a little like a planet," said Risa.

"A fat planet," said Willie.

"You said *Fang* was a space dog," said Gwen.

"He's in training for space, but he's a little high-strung," explained Colonel Castle. "I've been put in charge of the new animal training program."

"Willie and I are the only ones who can handle Fang without his muzzle," said Risa.

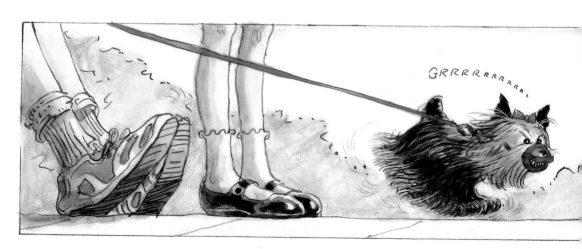

GRRRRRRRRR

ACTUAL SALAMI

RECONSTITUTED SALAMI

"Can Fletcher eat salami in space?" asked Jill.

Fletcher opened both eyes at the word *salami*.

"Reconstituted salami," said Colonel Castle.

Fletcher closed his eyes. Fang gave a high-pitched bark.

"He probably likes reconstituted salami," said Gwen.

"Fang's a very light eater," said Willie.

Fletcher did something he almost never, ever did. From deep in his belly, he let out a low, menacing growl.

"Fletcher doesn't like light eaters," explained Jill.

As soon as summer vacation began, Gwen, Jill, and Fletcher flew to Houston to begin Fletcher's training. At the space center Colonel Castle led them to a training room. Fang was on a treadmill. The little dog's legs were going as fast as they could. "Good job, Fang," said Colonel Castle.

Jill tied a piece of salami to the front of a treadmill for Fletcher, and Colonel Castle set the speed to medium.

After a while, everybody heard panting. The treadmill was going so fast poor Fletcher could barely keep up.

Jill turned off his machine. Fletcher lay down, exhausted. "Fletcher thinks running is for people, not dogs," she explained.

Gwen studied the speed control on Fletcher's machine. It was on high. "Who turned up Fletcher's treadmill?" she asked, tapping her braces. Gwen always tapped her braces when something queer was going on.

(CLOSE-UP OF CONTROL)

"Do you have something in your teeth?" asked Willie.

The next day Colonel Castle and Ms. Watsuda put Fletcher in the antigravity chamber. "May we try it?" asked Gwen.

Ms. Watsuda smiled. "Why not?"
"Wow!" said Gwen as she rolled up the wall.
"I can do a double somersault," said Jill. She held Fletcher up with one finger.

The door to the antigravity chamber opened. Risa and Fang entered. Fang wasn't wearing his muzzle.

Fang bared his teeth and tried to bite Fletcher. "Stop, Fang!" shrieked Risa.

Jill grabbed a Velcro leash from the side of the chamber. She got the leash on Fletcher and pulled him out of the way of Fang's teeth.

Once they were safely out, Gwen yelled at Risa, "Fletcher could have been killed."

"I didn't know you were in there," said Risa. "The sign on the chamber said Empty."

Gwen tapped her braces. "First the treadmill, then someone put the wrong sign…"

TAP
TAP
TAP
TAP
TAP
TAP
TAP
TAP
TAP
TAP
TAP
TAP
TAP
TAP

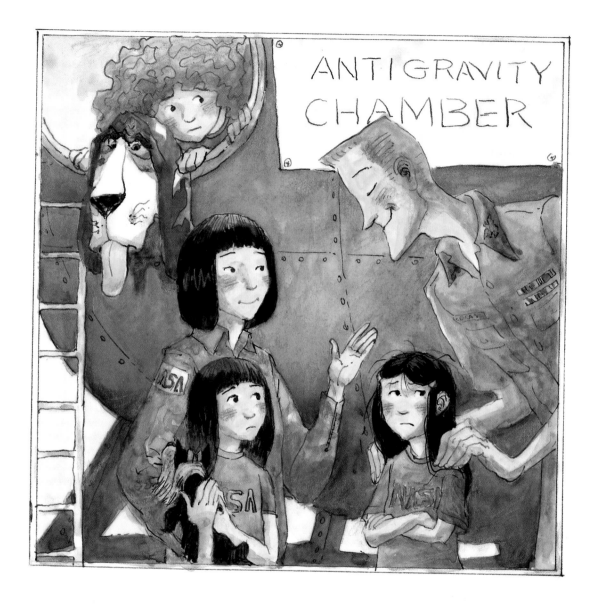

"Now, now," said Colonel Castle. "These little snafus happen. Take it from me."

"Colonel Castle should know," said Ms. Watsuda. "He was in training to be the next astronaut in space before they decided to use a dog instead."

Colonel Castle put his arm around Gwen. "Don't you worry. I'll look into these glitches."

Fletcher did extremely well on the eating part of his training. He definitely loved space ice cream and learned to take the foil off for himself. However, he still didn't like space salami. It was too bland.

NOTE: SPACE ICE CREAM IS FREEZE-DRIED, SO IT DOES NOT HAVE TO BE KEPT IN A FREEZER. IT'S NOT COLD.

Fletcher made rapid progress in his other training, too. "I never thought you'd whip that fat dog into shape," the chief engineer said to Colonel Castle.

Jill frowned. She didn't like Fletcher being called "that fat dog."

Finally, the day of Fletcher's launch arrived. Television crews from around the world came to meet the dog who looked like the planet earth and was going into space.

"He looks like he's asleep," said one of the reporters. "Deep down, he's very excited," said Jill.

Ms. Watsuda helped put Fletcher in the space capsule. Jill gave him a kiss on his nose. The door to the space capsule closed.

"Ten, nine, eight, seven, six, five, four, three, two, ONE! We have blast-off!" shouted the chief engineer. Jill held on to Gwen's hand as the rocket climbed through the clouds.

HT, SIEBEN, SECHS, FÜNF, VIER, DREI, ZWEI, EINS...DIECI, NOVE, OTTO, SETTE, SEI, CINQUE,

QUATTRO, TRE, DUE, UNO... ナ, カ, 九, 七, 六, 五, 四, 三, 二, 一...X, IX, VIII, VII, VI, V, IV, III, II, I

FLETCHER

Gwen and Jill watched Fletcher on the monitor. His ears, no longer pulled down by gravity, floated out to the side like two flying carpets.

Fletcher looked down and saw the boot of Italy and the coast of North Africa. They looked exactly like his right ear except Italy was green and brown and the Mediterranean Sea was blue.

He looked up and saw the day turning to night. The Milky Way looked close enough to lick.

Jill and Gwen spoke to Fletcher through their headsets. "You're passing Turkey!" said Jill. Fletcher wagged his tail.

"He likes countries that sound like food," Jill explained to the reporters.

"Uh-oh!" said the chief engineer.

The entire room grew quiet. *Uh-oh!* was the scariest word in the space program. "What's wrong?" asked Jill.

"I'm getting a weird reading from the medical sensors. There's another life-form in the space capsule."

"An alien!" shrieked Jill. Fletcher whimpered.

Gwen tapped
her braces. High-
pitched sounds
came through
space. "Yip, yip,
yip," went the
alien. "Tap, tap,
tap," went Gwen.
She pointed to
the sleeping bag.
"It's lumpy!"
she shouted.

YIP! YIP! YIP! YIP! YIP! YIP! YIP! YIP! YIP! YIP! YIP! (WALL SPEAKERS FOR SOUNDS FROM THE CAPSULE)

   "So Fletcher didn't make the bed," said Colonel Castle.
The chief engineer chuckled. Gwen didn't think it
was funny.

TAP-TAP-TAP-TAP-TAP-TAP-TAP-TAP-TAP-TAP-TAP-TAP-TAP-TAP-TAP-TAP-TAP-TAP-TAP-TAP-TAP-TAP

"We're getting two heartbeats—strange noises," said the chief engineer.

Jill shuddered. Gwen put her arm around her.

The space capsule hurtled through the night. Children in Singapore, Kyoto, and Perth turned on their lights as a way of saying hello to Fletcher.

But Fletcher wasn't looking out the window or thinking about food. His eyes were glued to the sleeping bag. It was twitching.

Every time the alien yipped or yapped, Gwen tapped.
"Yip, tap, yip, tap." It drove everybody crazy. Finally
Gwen looked around. "Where's Fang?" she asked.

"He's in his room," said Willie, "right below the
command center."
"I think we'd better check," said Gwen.

Everything in Fang's room was in place except Fang's leash and muzzle. And Fang!

"Where is he?" Jill demanded.

"I think I know," said Gwen. "We've got to get back to the command center."

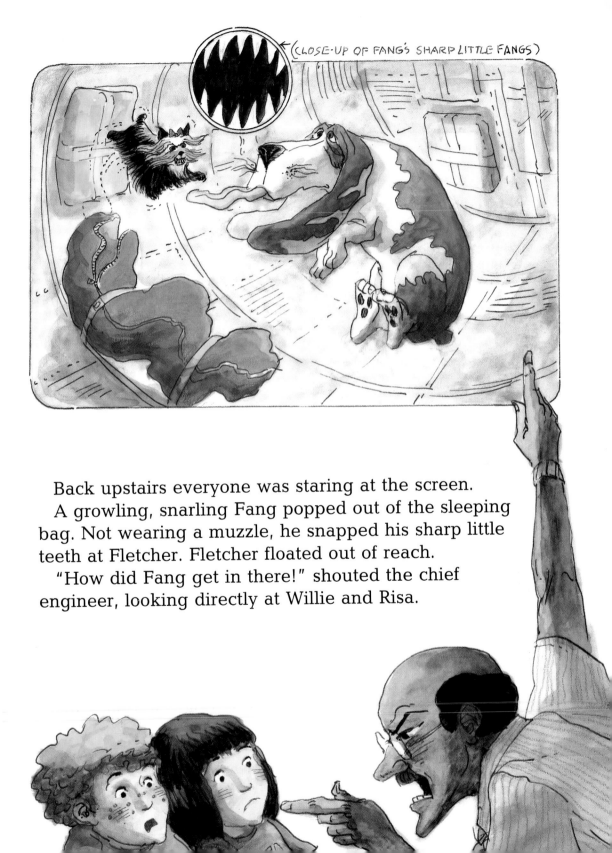

(CLOSE-UP OF FANG'S SHARP LITTLE FANGS)

Back upstairs everyone was staring at the screen.

A growling, snarling Fang popped out of the sleeping bag. Not wearing a muzzle, he snapped his sharp little teeth at Fletcher. Fletcher floated out of reach.

"How did Fang get in there!" shouted the chief engineer, looking directly at Willie and Risa.

"It wasn't Risa or me," said Willie.

"I know," said Gwen.

"What do you mean?" shrieked Jill. "Willie and Risa have been trying to sabotage Fletcher's mission since day one."

Gwen shook her head. "You're wrong, but we can't deal with that now. We've got to save Fletcher."

"Tell Fang to stay!" Gwen yelled to Willie.

"Stay, Fang!" commanded Willie.

"We'll never keep those two dogs apart," moaned Colonel Castle. "They *hate* each other."

"With Willie on the headset to Fang and Jill talking to Fletcher, those two dogs won't hurt each other," said Gwen.

"Oh yeah?" said the chief engineer. "What about reentry? The outside of the space capsule gets so hot, all radio communication and transmissions are cut."

"They'll kill each other," said Jill and Willie.

The sun rose over California while Jill and Willie stayed on their headsets, talking to Fang and Fletcher, telling them to keep apart.

Gwen slowly circled the command center, tapping her braces. She got down on all fours.

"Stop being silly," pleaded Jill. "I'm really scared about Fletcher's reentry."

"I'm not being silly," said Gwen. "*Now* I'm solving the mystery."

"We have to fire the retro-rockets," said the chief engineer. The air around the capsule glowed a fiery pink as it slammed back into the earth's atmosphere.

Then the screen went blank. The earphones went dead. The TV screen was nothing but streaks of black and white. "That's probably dog fur," said Willie forlornly.

"Fletcher just didn't have enough training. He's panicking," said Colonel Castle.

"Not enough training, or does he have an enemy in space?" interrupted Gwen.

"Gwen," whispered Jill, "you're talking to an astronaut."

"An astronaut, but not a nice man," said Gwen, tapping her braces.

"What are you talking about?" asked the chief engineer.

"Something queer in outer space!" shouted Gwen. "And it started right down here on earth."

"She's just a little girl," protested Colonel Castle, laughing.

The chief engineer wasn't smiling. "Go on, Gwen," he said.

SLEEPING BAG

←MUZZLE

"At first I thought it was Willie and Risa. Then I thought it could be you." The chief engineer looked shocked. "You thought Fletcher was too fat for space," continued Gwen.

"Fang can't go anywhere without his muzzle," explained Gwen, "except with Willie and Risa. Colonel Castle used the muzzle to put him in the space-capsule sleeping bag. Then he took the muzzle off so that Fang would scare Fletcher and ruin his mission."

"I think she left her brain floating in the antigravity chamber," chuckled Colonel Castle.

"Then how do you account for Fang's dog hair on your crisp, clean uniform," said Gwen, holding up a strand of Fang's long, sleek fur that she had found on Colonel Castle's pants leg.

"Space belongs to people, not dogs *or* little girls. I order you kids out of the command center!" shouted Colonel Castle.

Jill looked up at the screen. "I can't leave Fletcher!" she wailed.

"Get out now!" commanded Colonel Castle. He lunged for Gwen. Gwen ducked under the computers.

"Stop it, John!" shouted Ms. Watsuda.

Suddenly everybody heard a munching sound. "It sounds like someone's being chewed to death!" said the chief engineer, listening on his earphones to the sounds from the space capsule.

"Oh, Fletcher," wailed Jill. "Fang's eating him."

"Or vice versa," sniffed Risa.

The picture cleared. "What the...," exclaimed the chief engineer. Fletcher and Fang were both wagging their tails and chewing something, but it wasn't each other.

"Fletcher!" cried Jill.

"Fang!" cried Willie.

"What are they eating?" demanded Gwen, tapping her braces.

The camera zoomed out.

"It's salami!" said Gwen. "Real salami. Did you put it there, Jill?"

Jill shook her head.

"How did Fletcher get salami in space?" asked Jill.

Gwen started to tap her braces. "A planet made of salami?"

SALAMI PLANET

SEEDED-ROLL MOON

RINGS OF MUSTARD AND PICKLE SLICES

BAGEL MOON

Risa giggled softly. "I felt sorry for Fletcher," she whispered, "having to go up into space without real salami."

"Those dogs should never have gone up in the first place," muttered Colonel Castle. "That's why I sneaked Fang in. I wanted to show everybody what a disaster it would be."

"John," said Ms. Watsuda, "you've got it all wrong. Space is big enough for animals and people."

Colonel Castle flashed a dirty look at Gwen and stomped out of the command center.

Gwen looked up into space. The parachutes had opened. Fletcher and Fang flipped and floated and did a fandango back to earth.

(THE FANDANGO IS A FIERY SPANISH DANCE)

"How did they go up as enemies and come down as friends?" asked Jill in an awed voice.

Gwen tapped her braces, but she was stumped. Some mysteries in space were too deep even for Gwen.